Beautiful OHIO

OF THE NORTHWEST TERRITORIES

JOHN TUDOR

Primix Publishing
East Brunswick Office Evolution
1 Tower Center Boulevard, Ste 1510
East Brunswick, NJ 08816
www.primixpublishing.com
Phone: 1-800-538-5788

Published by Primix Publishing: 12/18/2024

ISBN: 979-8-89194-310-0(sc)
ISBN: 979-8-89194-311-7(e)

Library of Congress Control Number: 2024918702

Contents

To the reader, Welcome aboard!

We will explore the beautiful state of Ohio starting from early times to present times. I hope the trip makes you aware of those things that make Ohio wonderful. Incidentally, the first chapter is on prehistoric Ohio. If you are among those that loathe prehistoric discussions, please feel free to skip chapter 1 and go directly to chapter 2. No one will hold this against you.

PREHISTORIC OHIO

OVER THE YEARS, THE LAND that is now Ohio—particularly the northern part—was repeatedly impacted by glacial movements. These glaciers carried soil, stones, and possibly even seeds from the northern regions as they advanced southward. While subsequent glaciers often erased evidence of their predecessors, the final glacier left a lasting mark. For instance, as it moved down from the north, it covered the area now occupied by Lake Erie. The glacier pushed the lake south, establishing a new southern boundary that ran approximately along an east-west line through Findlay. When the glacier eventually receded, the lake returned to its original location but left behind a 'south shoreline.' Though much of this shoreline has since been erased by modern agriculture and other land use, some sections remain easily traceable, marking the period when Lake Erie, under the glacier's pressure, temporarily settled at this new southern limit.

Later, as the glacier began to melt, the meltwater ran off primarily to the east and south. The routes of the melting water included the Maumee River, which flowed westward, likely following the Wabash watercourse in Indiana before joining the Ohio River and eventually the Mississippi, near Cairo, Illinois. At that time, this region was the northern reach of the

Gulf of Mexico. Another major recipient of meltwater was the St. Lawrence waterway, which flowed eastward through the Niagara River, into what is now known as Lake Ontario, and ultimately into the St. Lawrence River, carrying the water to the Atlantic Ocean.

The Maumee River once carried meltwater southwest from the Toledo area, but today it flows in the opposite direction—from the confluence of the St. Joseph and St. Mary's Rivers—northeast through Toledo into Lake Erie. I recall an interesting moment from my undergraduate days in the 'Reserve Officers Training Corps.' Our instructor, a retired Army major, was lecturing on aerial map reading and taught us that you can always determine a river's flow direction by noting the orientation of its tributaries as they join the main river. While generally useful advice, it raised questions about the Maumee River, which now flows northeast into Lake Erie, with its tributaries pointing in the opposite direction. This anomaly puzzled the class until we understood that the Maumee River once carried meltwater from the glacier but later reversed its flow to carry local water toward Lake Erie.

Fortuitously, there was a large map of the area hanging on the wall behind him. When I pointed out the Maumee's exception to his rule, the instructor realized that his guideline had probable local exceptions. As you might expect from a retired major, he didn't appreciate being corrected, but the class certainly enjoyed it.

Most geological features created by earlier glaciers were largely destroyed by the glaciers that followed. However, the last glacier left two distinct but similarly formed monuments marking its presence. The first is the terminal moraine, a ridge of land and stones pushed up by the glacier at the point where it stopped advancing.

The second feature was created by the glacier's meltwater. As the water flowed off the glacier into rivers both on and near the ice, the riverbanks were often made of ice themselves. While these rivers helped drain the meltwater, they also deposited dirt and other debris that the glacier had scraped up during its southward journey. When the glacier receded and the ice rivers no longer carried water, the accumulated sediment settled, forming ridges where the rivers once flowed. These ridges, known as eskers, are still visible in some areas today.

Repeat of Chapter 1 for those who just woke up.

As the glacier melted, it relieved the tremendous weight pressing down on the land beneath it. This allowed the land to slowly rise, which caused the Maumee River to reverse its flow. The St. Mary's and St. Joseph Rivers, which merge at Fort Wayne, now flow northeast as the Maumee does today. Traditionally, aerial map readers are taught that rivers flow in the same direction their tributaries point downstream. However, this is not true of the Maumee River, which reversed its flow after the glacier melted in the Toledo area.

Before this reversal, the Maumee served as a major channel for glacial meltwater, flowing southwestward—possibly into what we now know as the Wabash River, which eventually joined the Ohio River. The Ohio River, in turn, flows into the Mississippi River just below Cairo, Illinois. Contrary to some assumptions, the Mississippi meets the Gulf of Mexico at New Orleans, not at Cairo.

Chapter 2

THE MOUNDBUILDERS

THE AREA NOW KNOWN AS Ohio was sparsely populated before the immigration of the Moundbuilders, likely from the Valley of Mexico, and by the Archaic people around 10,000 to 12,000 years ago. These early inhabitants did not form what scholars would classify as a 'culture.' However, the melting of the last glacier, particularly in the southern part of Ohio near the Scioto River, gave rise to the first identifiable culture in the region: the Glacier Kame people. They occupied the northwestern part of Ohio, which includes the area around present-day Toledo.

Most of Ohio was sparsely inhabited by the Adena culture, which would eventually be absorbed by the Hopewell culture. The Adena were known for creating small burial mounds across the state, with perhaps only one to two hundred mounds in total. They also constructed a few larger mounds, including the famous Serpent Mound, shaped like a serpent, and the Graves Creek Mound to the northeast.

The Adena built houses in Ohio and also occupied lands south of the Ohio River, extending 50 to 100 miles beyond it. Their homes were constructed by setting posts in a circular pattern and covering them with bark or other materials. This building method may have been a precursor to the pole barns commonly seen today.

By the time Native Americans began to populate Ohio, the Moundbuilders were migrating primarily northeastward, leaving their mounds behind. These mounds served mainly as burial sites. The deceased were often cremated, but due to the limitations of early cremation methods, many skeletons survived the process. They were sometimes buried in timber boxes, which remain intact to this day.

Unfortunately, most of the mounds have been disturbed by individuals seeking artifacts, as well as by agriculture, industry, and housing development. However, a few of the larger mounds remain preserved, including the Serpent Mound, which is located in a state park of the same name.

The Adena culture developed significant manufacturing skills, often crafting copper items, including strips for personal protection and breastplates. They appeared to wear elk antlers, either taken from the skulls of elk or created through other means, and fashioned helmets adorned with copper antlers.

Many of the mounds can be found along the Scioto River in southern Ohio, including in the Beacon Valley. In total, 134 mounds have been identified in Ohio, primarily constructed by the Adena culture. Among the notable surviving mounds are the five Miller mounds, the Serpent Mound, and various works in Ross County, including the corm mounds at Athens, Ohio.

Unlike the Egyptians, who built pyramids using slave labor, the mounds of the Moundbuilders were constructed over time by people who volunteered to bury their kin and maintain the mounds. This communal effort is reflected in the layered construction of the mounds, indicating that they were built over an extended period. A well-preserved area of such mounds can be found at Mound wood near Indian Lake in Logan County, although they are now largely covered by mature trees.

The Moundbuilders were the earliest people to leave a recognizable memorial of their existence in Ohio. They constructed numerous mounds across the state, some of which have been farmed over and destroyed, while others remain in wooded areas or are preserved in state parks. These early inhabitants are referred to as the 'Adena Culture' or the 'Glacial Kame People.'

These mounds were built for various purposes, including burial sites, ceremonial structures, and venues for social and religious gatherings. The Adena Culture, for example, constructed large earthworks that often served as burial mounds, interring the remains of important individuals along with artifacts such as pottery, tools, and ornaments. Other mounds may have been created to mark territorial boundaries or to facilitate astronomical observations, aligning with celestial events. The significance of these mounds reflects the complex spiritual and social lives of the Moundbuilders, and their construction showcases the impressive organizational skills of these early peoples.

Warriors, including notable leaders such as Tecumseh and Cornstalk, entered the Ohio country unopposed, making their way into the region from the headlands of the Cumberland and Tennessee Rivers. These courageous individuals were members of the Shawnee tribe, along with various allies, and their arrival marked a significant moment in the history of Native American resistance against European encroachment.

Chapter 3

THE AMERICAN INDIANS IN OHIO

Tʜᴇ Oʜɪᴏ ᴄᴏᴜɴᴛʀʏ ᴡᴀs ʀɪᴄʜ in resources and strategically important, making it a focal point for both indigenous tribes and settlers. Tecumseh, a visionary leader, sought to unite various tribes to resist the advancing settlers and to reclaim their lands, which were being increasingly threatened. Cornstalk, known for his wisdom and military prowess, was also instrumental in rallying the tribes to stand together against the common threat.

As they moved through the lush landscapes of Ohio, these warriors were not just fighting for territory; they were defending their way of life and ensuring the survival of their cultures. Their presence and actions during this period were vital in shaping the dynamics of the region, illustrating the complex interplay of power, resistance, and survival in the face of external pressures. The legacy of Tecumseh, Cornstalk, and their fellow warriors continues to resonate in the historical narrative of the indigenous peoples of North America.

Cornstalk (c. 1727–1777), a Shawnee leader, played a significant role in defending Shawnee lands during British American expansion into the Ohio Country. Known in Shawnee as Hokoleskwa, he first appears in records as a hostage during peace talks after Pontiac's War in 1764. As war chief in Lord Dunmore's War (1774), Cornstalk led Shawnee forces at the Battle of Point Pleasant but later advocated for neutrality during the American Revolutionary War. In 1777, while on a diplomatic mission to Fort Randolph, he was imprisoned and later executed by American soldiers, enraging the Shawnees and silencing a key voice for peace.

During the time European explorers arrived, the Ohio area was sparsely occupied by various local tribes who lived primarily as hunter-gatherers or engaged in small-scale agriculture. Among these tribes were the Delaware, Miami, Shawnee, and Wyandot. Their way of life was intricately connected to the land, relying on the rich natural resources of Ohio.

The French laid claim to the Ohio region, largely based on the efforts of churchmen who sought to convert Native Americans to Christianity, as well as traders purchasing beaver skins from indigenous peoples. This claim was further established by French surveyors and explorers who ventured into the territory. By around 1790, traders from colonial America began to arrive, adding to the complex dynamics between European settlers and Native Americans. As colonial Americans sought to expand westward beyond the Allegheny Mountains, they faced resistance from the indigenous tribes, who were determined to protect their lands. The French attempted to prevent colonial Americans from encroaching on the territory, leading to increased tensions.

The struggle for control over the Ohio region culminated in significant conflict, particularly during the French and Indian War. This conflict, which had strong ties to larger European struggles, resulted in a substantial victory for the English and colonial forces. France ultimately ceded its claims to the land between the Appalachian Mountains and the Mississippi River to Great Britain.

Following the American War of Independence, formalized by the Treaty of Paris, the same territory ceded by France to Britain was granted to the newly established United States. However, efforts to dislodge the Native Americans from Northwest Ohio faced significant challenges. Three military expeditions aimed at removing the indigenous tribes from the area ultimately failed.The decisive moment came in the Battle of Fallen Timbers, where General Anthony Wayne led American forces to victory against British-backed Native American warriors, including those led by the notorious British general known as "the Hair Buyer." Tecumseh, a prominent Shawnee leader, suggested that the Native Americans turn and fight, which they did. Despite their bravery, the Native American forces, along with their British allies, were defeated. Tragically, Tecumseh was killed during this conflict, although his body was never found. This battle marked a significant turning point in the struggle for control over Ohio and the broader region, altering the course of history for both the Native American tribes and European settlers.

Chapter 4

EARLY CLAIMS OF SOVEREIGNTY OVER THE LAND OF OHIO

THE ANCIENTS DID NOT CLAIM any interest in North American land that they did not personally use or live on. It was the French who first claimed an interest in the land between the Allegheny Mountains and the Mississippi River. The basis for the French claim was about as tenable as Neil Armstrong's claim to certain power over the moon. This claim was largely rooted in the visit of French explorer LaSalle around 1669. Several years later, French traders and churchmen crisscrossed the land and waters in search of beaver pelts and souls, arguably putting the French ahead of others in making much out of very little. They didn't even raise a flag, but this claim was later challenged by war.

The conflict in Europe spilled over into the Americas and became known as the French and Indian War, even though the French and the Indians were allies. For some time, Native Americans had pushed back against English colonists trying to cross the western edge of the mountains. The treaty that ended the French and Indian War, signed in 1763, resulted in France ceding its interests in the land to Great Britain, including a couple of small French villages in Ohio. General George Rogers Clark visited these people and found them celebrating and dancing; he simply advised them that "they were now dancing under the flag of the Americans," and they were okay with that. This development placed America's claim to Ohio on par with those of the French and the British.

The Treaty of Paris, which concluded the War of American Independence from Great Britain, granted this vast territory to the victorious colonies, now referred to as 'states.' However, Britain did not withdraw its people from Ohio; instead, it incited Native Americans against the settlers from its headquarters in Detroit. As a result, the Americans had to reassert their rights granted by Britain in the Treaty of Paris. This situation highlighted Britain's longstanding habit of disregarding the rights of Native Americans as outlined in their treaty provisions.

The land lying north of the Ohio River was designated as the Northwest Territory and fell under the direct governance of the Confederation of the thirteen original states. In this context, the Congress of the Confederation notably adopted the Ordinance of 1787, which established a government appointed by Congress, consisting of a governor, a secretary, and a common law court. The governor would serve as the commander-in-chief of the militia if needed. Upon achieving a population of five thousand free male inhabitants of full age, each part of the territory seeking statehood would be considered on an equal basis with the original thirteen states.

To its lasting credit, the Confederation Congress enacted the Ordinance of 1787, which included provisions prohibiting slavery in the Northwest Territory. Prior to this, no state had ever been denied the use of slavery. When Ohio gained statehood in 1803 with this prohibition, it became the first state to constitutionally deny slavery. Following the approval of the Northwest Ordinance, all new states admitted thereafter would also be prohibited from exercising the power of slavery. Article VI states, "There shall be neither slavery nor involuntary servitude in the said territories (being the Northwest Territories)."

This enactment laid the foundation for bringing all future deserving northwest lands into statehood, fully endowed as the original thirteen but without slavery. In my opinion, the Ordinance of 1787 is as formative a document as the Declaration of Independence and the U.S. Constitution. It set the requirements and authority for all future areas to be admitted to statehood without slavery, including those later admitted from beyond the Northwest Territory.

Several of the original American colonies, now called "states," laid claim to land beyond the mountains and westward to the Mississippi River. Georgia claimed land that is now Alabama, while North Carolina asserted its claims all the way to the Mississippi River, which included present-day Tennessee. Virginia claimed territory extending to the Mississippi River, which became Kentucky, and Connecticut, bypassing New York, claimed the extreme northwest portion of Ohio. Although the colonies were now free from Great Britain, they were left with a significant war debt, as the war had largely been fought by militias of the various states rather than by George Washington's standing army.

Chapter 5

THE ARTICLES OF CONFEDERATION

THE NEW GOVERNMENT, ESTABLISHED UNDER the Articles of Confederation, needed a source of income. Consequently, a deal was struck whereby the states governed by the Articles of Confederation ceded their claims to western lands in exchange for the national government covering their war debts over time. Prior to this agreement, Virginia had set aside lands between the Scioto and Miami Rivers in Ohio to compensate soldiers who had not been fully paid. Connecticut established a "Firelands" to compensate its citizens whose homes had been burned by the British during the War of Independence; this area was later moved to the western end of the Western Reserve.

These territories were excluded from the aforementioned deal. The land in northeastern Ohio, stretching through what is now Cleveland, was reserved for Virginia to pay its Revolutionary War soldiers and is still known as the Virginia Military Land Grants.

Having received the Northwest Territory and claimed the land south of the Ohio River, the federal government, under the Articles of Confederation, agreed to govern the Northwest Territory by dividing it into no more than seven states, including Ohio, as the area became sufficiently populated. Most growth began with the founding of Cleveland on Lake Erie in the north and Marietta at the confluence of the Ohio and Muskingum Rivers in the south. Once Ohio's population reached the required size, it was able to draft a state constitution and petition for statehood, which was granted in 1803. Ohio, serving as the gateway for settlement in the Northwest Territory, eventually led to the creation of five states and a portion of Minnesota from these lands.

As promised, Ohio became a state of the United States, endowed with every power of the original thirteen states except for the ownership of slaves, thanks to the wisdom of the Ordinance of 1787. The state's population exploded rapidly. For instance, Pittsburgh became a hub for constructing flat-bottom riverboats, which were ideal for pioneers floating down the Ohio River to their chosen tributaries where they intended to settle. The Welsh established a community at Paddy's Run (near Lebanon) along the Great Miami River, while Virginians navigated the Scioto River, creating a significant benefit for the unpaid Virginia militiamen.

In northeastern Ohio, pioneers faced unreliable currents on Lake Erie but launched a paddleboat named "Walk in the Water." There were fears that the new state of Ohio would be dominated by Virginians, which could control the government at statehood. This concern led to delays in establishing a new state government, but Ohio quickly became the 17th state in 1803.

With Virginians in control, the capital was established first at Circleville, then moved to Chillicothe, and finally to a new city being built along the Scioto River—Columbus. The state was firmly in the hands of the people from southern Ohio rather than those from northeastern Ohio. Once Ohio proposed a democratic state constitution to Congress and applied for statehood, Congress swiftly granted it. Ohio was clearly the gateway to the Northwest Territory and was active in governance, electing Edward Tiffin as its first governor, along with a clear majority of southern Ohioans in the state legislature.

We pause here to highlight a remarkable and perhaps unusual fact about the growth of governments. The new Americans who occupied the colonies along the eastern coast of what would become the United States—from Maine to Georgia—quickly recognized that the United States was destined to grow into a vast nation, spanning from one ocean to the other and populated by individuals who were not only British by birth but also included a diverse array of immigrants from various backgrounds.

Despite this understanding, they consciously chose to empower the newcomers who would fill the expanding country. This was evident in the Articles of Confederation, which would eventually evolve into the Constitution of the United States. Article II clearly states that each state retains sovereignty, freedom, and independence, along with all powers not expressly delegated to the United States Congress. This principle is echoed in the 10th Amendment to the Constitution, which asserts that "the powers not delegated to the United States by the Constitution, nor prohibited by it to the States, are reserved to the States respectively, or to the people."

By granting equal powers to the new states as enjoyed by the original thirteen, the founding generation willingly transferred control to the new Americans who would shape the future of the nation. In essence, the original colonies relinquished their grip on power to facilitate the growth of a prosperous country, recognizing that the new states would not merely be "second-class citizens." The early settlers were not intent on creating "a little England in America." They understood that future generations of Americans would emerge from a diverse population that included individuals beyond their own European roots.

The historical lesson is clear: those who establish a new government and democratically organize a nation do not need to remain the sole custodians of power. A new country can embrace a variety of backgrounds, as long as the foundational concepts of democracy are preserved. The immigration of non-English speakers and individuals of different colors and backgrounds can successfully enrich a democratic and powerful nation, enabling it to expand and assimilate new citizens who share the dreams envisioned by the original European founders.

Chapter 6

THE NORTHWEST TERRITORIES

After the Treaty of Paris concluded the War of American Independence, Great Britain ceded the entire area to the new nation. The region north of the Ohio River was designated as the Northwest Territory. Traders from both Virginia and Pennsylvania illegally entered and conducted business in this territory, while many states with open land beyond their western boundaries claimed rights to the territory extending to the Mississippi River. Georgia laid claim to Alabama and the Mississippi River, North Carolina claimed Tennessee, Virginia claimed Kentucky, and Connecticut, leaping over New York, asserted its claim to an area in Northeast Ohio known as the Western Reserve.

Following the War of Independence, the larger states faced substantial war debts, and the nation was governed under the Articles of Confederation. These Articles were eventually replaced by the adoption of the Constitution of the United States in 1789. The states operating under the Articles needed land for expansion, and the major colonies required assistance in settling their debts. To address this, a deal was structured whereby all colonies relinquished their claims to western lands in favor of the confederation government, which in turn would assume their debts.

Virginia claimed a significant tract of land in southern Ohio to compensate for its unpaid war debts, specifically the area between the Scioto River and the Miami River. Meanwhile, Great Britain, whose troops had a notorious history of setting fire to homes, designated an area in northwestern Ohio known as the Western Reserve. This area was referred to as "Firelands" because it was populated by many individuals who had lost their homes to British burning.

The land reserved for Virginia became known as the Virginia Military District, prompting the capital of Ohio to relocate to Chillicothe, a city in central Ohio, rather than remain in Cleveland, located in the northeast. However, there remained anxious Indigenous peoples in Ohio and settlers eager to annex federal lands for their homes, leading to conflicts. Treaties were signed but frequently broken by both sides, primarily by settlers whose homes were established in the Northwest Territory even before the government was ready to sell or provide proper deeds. Nevertheless, these issues were generally resolved, allowing settlers to retain their homes.

Ohio was the easternmost of all the new states that constituted the Northwest Territory. It met the population and other criteria for statehood and was admitted as the 17th state of the Union in 1803. Other future states that emerged from the Northwest Territory included Indiana, Illinois, Michigan, Wisconsin, and Minnesota—essentially comprising a geographical area similar to that of the Big Ten football league when I was in high school.

The amalgamation of the thirteen original colonies had to be accomplished swiftly and effectively after the successful War of American Independence. Much work was required to create a harmonious and unified new country. This effort was initiated by members of Congress, acting as "delegates of the thirteen states," who adopted the Articles of Confederation and Perpetual Union on July 9, 1778, in the third year of independence, as the states sought to strengthen their union. The Articles were signed by "We the undersigned delegates of the States," affirming that "the Articles of Confederation are perpetually a union between the states."

In contrast, the Constitution of the United States begins with "We the people of the United States, in order to form a more perfect union... do ordain and establish this Constitution." This difference is significant; the Constitution grants power to the United States by the people, who affix their names to a perpetual union among the states. In short, the Constitution is created by the people delegating powers to the central government, while the Articles of Confederation merely outline a perpetual union between the states, signed not by the people themselves but by the chosen delegates of the thirteen original colonies.

This arrangement was inherently flawed, particularly because the federal government lacked the power to levy and collect a national income tax.

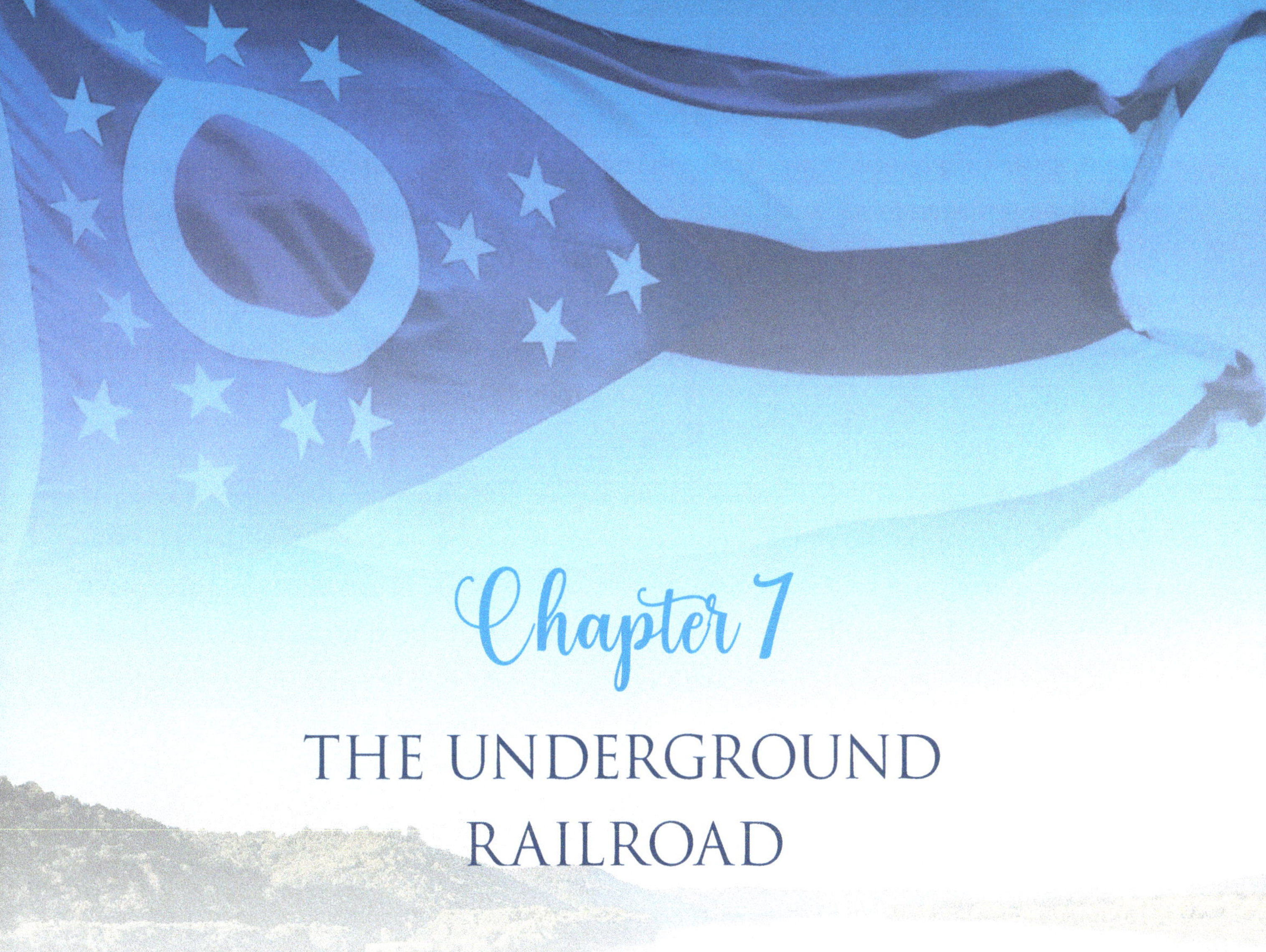

Chapter 7

THE UNDERGROUND RAILROAD

WHILE OHIO WAS PREPARING TO apply for statehood, the western lands of Virginia, recently acquired from Great Britain as part of the settlement of the War for American Independence, were admitted as the 15th state, Kentucky. Kentucky's territory extended south of the low water line of the Ohio River, meaning that the river itself became part of Kentucky but was never part of the Northwest Territories. Consequently, Kentucky accepted slavery, whereas slavery was forever prohibited in Ohio by the Northwest Ordinance, adopted by the Confederation Congress on July 13, 1787, before Ohio achieved statehood. This ordinance served as a kind of precursor to Ohio's constitution.

Kentucky, already a state by then, retained the full power to decide on the issue of slavery. Its decision to allow slavery extended that institution to the northern shore of the Ohio River, a sharp contrast to Ohio, where slavery was banned.

The Underground Railroad was neither underground nor a railroad, but rather an organization of "conductors" who helped enslaved people escape slavery. These conductors guided them northward, primarily to free states like Ohio, and in some cases, all the way to Canada. Along the way, they provided safe havens, often hiding the fugitives in basements or outbuildings for a night or two before conducting them to the next safe location. This complex and dangerous operation was further complicated by the federal government's adoption of the **Fugitive Slave Act,** which empowered slaveholders to legally reclaim escaped slaves. The law established a legal process whereby even those who had reached free states could be forced to return to slavery. Despite the risks, Underground Railroad conductors worked diligently to keep escapees hidden and out of reach of slave catchers, maintaining secrecy and aiding freedom seekers in their perilous journey north.

The perception that individuals escaping slavery were safe once they crossed into the Northwest Territories was, in fact, misleading. Despite being in free states, they were still vulnerable to being captured and returned to slave states, as stipulated by the **Fugitive Slave Act.** This meant that a newly freed person could be forcibly returned to their former owner or sold at a slave auction, even after reaching a free state. The issue persisted until the adoption of the **14th Amendment** to the U.S. Constitution, which declared that "No state shall make or enforce any law which shall abridge the privileges or immunities of citizens of the United States." This amendment ensured that the rights and freedoms of individuals could not be overridden by state laws, effectively protecting those who had escaped slavery. As a result, the symbolic importance of the Ohio River as the "American River Jordan" — once seen as a boundary between slavery and freedom — began to fade, as crossing it no longer guaranteed escape from the reach of oppressive laws.

The patience and resilience of enslaved individuals and former slaves in their pursuit of full citizenship and equality is truly remarkable. Their unwavering belief that they would one day be embraced as full citizens, without exception, speaks to their strength of character and hope for a better future. I once knew a Black businessman who demonstrated a powerful sense of patriotism when he caught a young child defacing the American flag. With conviction, he told the child, "You have lots of freedom, but don't deface my flag." In that moment, the flag wasn't just a symbol of a country—it was *his* flag, representing the hard-fought freedoms of all Americans, including himself and his ancestors. The child's lesson was clear, and from then on, he never again misused the flag. The businessman's deep respect for "Old Glory" was a testament to the enduring faith in the ideals of freedom and equality, even in the face of adversity.

Chapter 8

PERRY'S NAVAL BATTLE

A T THE TIME OF THE War of 1812, the British navy was, without a doubt, the largest and strongest in the world. Maritime traffic on Lake Erie was growing rapidly, but no other country had a military presence on the lake, which provided access to the upper Great Lakes, including Lake Huron, Lake Michigan, Lake Superior, and Lake St. Clair. The British had free rein over Lake Erie, a significant advantage for them and a major disadvantage for other countries, especially the United States, which sought to conduct business in Ohio and enhance its military production.

Under the leadership of Rhode Island seaman and businessman Oliver Hazard Perry, a well-organized effort was made to build a new navy. A good supply of building materials and sailors was assembled, and a training base was established in the northwest corner of Pennsylvania. This location, particularly near Presque Isle, was ideal for boat building and shallow-water naval maneuvers. The boats constructed on Lake Erie were designed to suit the shallow waters where the battles would be fought, unlike the British ships, which were built for deeper water combat.

The decisive naval engagement occurred at Put-In-Bay, near the mainland town of Port

Clinton, Ohio. What began as a standard naval confrontation turned into a much larger conflict than either side had anticipated. The British were lured into the shallow, swampy waters, where their ships became vulnerable. In the ensuing battle, many sailors from both sides perished, and their names are now inscribed inside the Perry International Peace Monument, erected after the battle to commemorate peace on the Great Lakes. This monument symbolizes the enduring peace between nations, as no further military action has taken place on the Great Lakes since the British withdrew their ships.

During the battle, Perry's flagship was disabled, forcing him to transfer to another American vessel under heavy fire. In the end, the British were forced to surrender their entire fleet, marking a significant American victory. Oliver Hazard Perry emerged as a celebrated naval commander. It is said that this was the only time in history that an entire British naval squadron surrendered to its enemy. Today, Put-In-Bay is a popular destination for vacationers and university students, drawn by the historical significance of the battle.

Chapter 9

BEGINNINGS OF THE
NEW STATE OF OHIO

THE TRANSITION FROM GOVERNANCE UNDER the Articles of Confederation to the Constitution of the United States was a necessary step toward achieving the federal strength and revenue required to support a new democratic government without undermining its fragile foundations. While the Articles provided a framework for governance, the challenges they presented made effective management difficult. However, they did outline that "all charges and expenses incurred for common defense or general welfare, allowed by the United States and Congress assembled, shall be defrayed out of a common treasury," funded by the states in proportion to the value of all lands within their borders.

As the nation sought to establish a government perceived as democratic and duly elected, it harkened back to a time when many citizens could neither read nor write. To affirm their authority, individuals would often attach their personal seals to documents. This practice underscored the significance of representation and governance.

In this context, the legislative authority appointed four or five men to gather at the home of Thomas Worthington, near Chillicothe, to design a suitable state seal. This meeting reflected the human element of governance, embodying the belief that divine providence guided their efforts. However, the gathering quickly devolved into a card game, and before they realized it, dawn had arrived with little progress made toward creating a great seal.

Noticing the rising sun, Thomas Worthington stepped outside to his patio and reassured his fellow legislators, stating that there was no cause for concern. He pointed out the pastoral landscape surrounding them, highlighting the mountains, wheat stalks, and other symbols of agriculture that could be incorporated into the seal. This inspiration led to the design of the Great Seal of Ohio, which was crafted to represent the state's agricultural significance. The legislature approved the proposed seal, believing it would aptly reflect the affairs of the state and its commitment to agricultural prosperity.

When Congress convened to select a distinguished assembly of wise men to propose changes and improvements to the Articles of Confederation, the need for enhanced taxation powers was a clear priority. The delegates, who would later be regarded as our constitutional fathers, recognized the necessity for clearer articulation of governance and ultimately crafted a new Constitution. This document was presented to all thirteen states and, despite the drafters' deviation from established protocols to meet urgent needs, it was ultimately approved.

Additionally, the Confederation Congress drew upon the Ordinance of 1787, which prohibited slavery in all new states admitted to the Union. This ordinance also established provisions for substantial land allocations to ensure proper education for children and included a range of other grants necessary for the effective exercise of governmental power. In many meaningful ways, the Ordinance of 1787 aligns with the Declaration of Independence and the United States Constitution, serving as foundational pillars of our nation's structure.

The seal of Ohio beautifully illustrates the state's diverse geography and rich history. In the background, Mount Logan, located in Ross County, rises prominently. Separating Mount Logan from the other elements of the seal is the winding Scioto River. A freshly harvested wheat field features a wheat bushel, symbolizing Ohio's significant contributions to agriculture. Flanking the wheat bushel are 17 arrows, representing Ohio's status as the 17th state to join the Union. Above these elements, the sun shines with 13 rays, commemorating the original 13 colonies.

The concept for the Ohio seal originated in the early 1800s, likely inspired by the eastern view from Thomas Worthington's home, Adena, situated near present-day Chillicothe. Worthington, Ohio's first United States senator, also served as the state's sixth governor, further cementing his legacy in Ohio's history.

Adena was the 2,000-acre estate of Thomas Worthington (1773–1827), the sixth governor of Ohio and one of the state's first United States Senators. The mansion, completed in 1807, has been meticulously restored to reflect its original appearance during the Worthington family's residence, featuring many of their original furnishings.

The house is one of only three designed by the renowned architect Benjamin Henry Latrobe that still stands in the country today.

Nestled within the remaining 300 acres of the estate are five outbuildings and beautifully landscaped formal gardens, which have undergone significant renovations. Visitors can wander through three terraces filled with flowers and vegetables, as well as enjoy the shrubs and trees in the grove.

From the north lawn of the mansion, guests can gaze eastward across the Scioto River valley to the Logan Range, a view that inspired the design of the Great Seal of the State of Ohio.

The territory and the national government were designed to ensure that new states held the same powers as the original states, with authority ultimately passing to the new Americans.

 The thirteen original colonies wisely relinquished control to facilitate the growth of what would soon become a vast and diverse nation. Their focus was not on power struggles but on fostering a flourishing society for all citizens.

Early settlers envisioned a country where everyone could contribute to nation-building using their unique skills and interests. As new states were gradually admitted to the Union from the Northwest Territory, Indiana, Illinois, Michigan, Wisconsin, and Minnesota joined Ohio, which became one of the most populous states in the country. Remarkably, eight out of the next ten presidents hailed from Ohio, including Benjamin Harrison, who, although elected from Indiana, was born and raised in Ohio.

The amalgamation of the thirteen original colonies had to be accomplished swiftly and effectively after the successful War of American Independence. There was much work to do to unify the new country harmoniously. This effort was undertaken by members of Congress, serving as "delegates of the thirteen states," who adopted the Articles of Confederation and Perpetual Union on July 9, 1778, in the third year of independence. At this point, the states were still independent but aimed to come together in a stronger union.

The Articles were signed with the declaration, "We the undersigned delegates of the States affix our greetings that the Articles of Confederation are perpetually a union between the states." In contrast, the Constitution of the United States begins with, "We the People of the United States, in Order to form a more perfect Union, do ordain and establish this Constitution…" In essence, the Constitution contains powers granted to the federal government by the people, whereas the Articles of Confederation served as a framework for a government to which delegates affixed their names, creating a perpetual union between the states.

In short, the Constitution was crafted by the people, delegating powers to the central government, while the Articles of Confederation represented a statement of perpetual union among the states. The Constitution is a stable, irreversible coalition created by the populace, while the Articles were merely signed by the chosen delegates of the thirteen original colonies. This arrangement was inherently flawed, particularly since the federal government lacked the authority to impose and collect a national income tax.

The transition from governance under the Articles of Confederation to the Constitution of the United States was a necessary step toward strengthening federal authority and ensuring a stable income without jeopardizing the fragile nature of a democratically elected government. Under the Articles of Confederation, those tasked with governing the country faced challenges, but their efforts were not entirely ineffective. The Articles stipulated that "all charges and expenses incurred for common defense or general warfare allowed by the United States and Congress assembled shall be defrayed out of a common treasury," which would be supplied by the several states in proportion to the value of all lands within those states.

The establishment of this form of government was intended to be democratic and duly elected, reflecting the collective will of the people.

When Congress decided to convene a worthy assembly to propose changes and improvements to the Articles of Confederation, the need for enhanced taxation powers was clearly on the agenda. The group, known as the Constitutional Fathers, recognized that clarity and precision were essential. They drafted the Constitution, which was presented to all thirteen colonies and ultimately approved, despite the drafters departing from their strict procedural rules to meet the urgency of the moment.

Another significant achievement was the Confederation Congress's redrafting of the Ordinance of 1787, which prohibited slavery in all new states admitted to the Union. This ordinance also included provisions for setting aside substantial land to create educational opportunities for children and outlined various grants of necessary powers to ensure proper governance and security in exercising those powers. In many ways, the Ordinance of 1787 aligns with the principles of the Declaration of Independence and the United States Constitution, serving as a foundational element in the structure of our nation.

When Congress convened to propose improvements to the Articles of Confederation, the need for enhanced taxation powers was a central focus. The group known as the Constitutional Fathers recognized that greater clarity was essential. They drafted the Constitution, which was presented to all thirteen colonies and ultimately approved, despite the drafters deviating from their strict procedural rules to address the urgency of the situation.

Another significant achievement was the Confederation Congress's redrafting of the Ordinance of 1787, which prohibited slavery in all new states admitted to the Union. This ordinance also included provisions for setting aside substantial land to create educational opportunities for children, along with a comprehensive list of necessary powers and provisions to ensure effective governance and security in the exercise of those powers. In a meaningful way, the Ordinance of 1787 aligns with the principles of the Declaration of Independence and the United States Constitution, serving as foundational elements in the structure of our nation.

Chapter 10

A SUCCESSFUL UNION OF TWO NATIONALITIES

SOMETIMES, UNEXPECTED EVENTS LEAD TO beautiful solutions that are appreciated for years. A notable example involves a group of Welsh immigrants who set out for Pittsburgh with the intention of building boats to float down the Ohio River, which technically begins in Pittsburgh, to establish a new Welsh community on the Miami River near Lebanon, Ohio. However, they must have started their journey late, as they only made it to Gallipolis, a struggling little French village. Upon arrival, they were welcomed and informed that the community was in dire need of support. The French residents of Gallipolis (which means "City of the Galls") were living day by day but regularly losing inhabitants. They offered the Welsh the opportunity to stay and help save the town, promising that the community would treat them very well in return.

The Welsh expressed their gratitude for the generosity and kindness shown to them but decided to continue their journey the following day to the Welsh community downstream. However, a significant turn of events occurred: the Welsh had neglected to post guards on their boats. By morning, it became clear that someone had severed the ropes securing the vessels, leaving them adrift.

At that point, the Welsh realized they had been hasty in turning down the generosity of the French and, upon reflection, decided to join their community. This "marriage" proved to be beneficial, as the defense of the country required steel manufacturing—a skill the French lacked but the Welsh had mastered in their native land.

To this day, the Welsh and French collaborate closely, supporting the local bank, which has provided services to both communities and continues to thrive as The Oak Hill Bank. The French assisted the Welsh in establishing homes and employment opportunities, including the construction of kilns, which had previously created significant jobs back in Wales.

As the national government's need for steel grew for military defense, it paid handsomely for Welsh iron, contributing to their prosperity. Although no one ever came forward to claim responsibility for releasing the boats, several elderly residents insisted they saw an angel walking around the docks on the night the ropes were untied.

Chapter 11

MEET SOME GREAT OHIOANS

OHIO QUICKLY ADOPTED THE NEEDS of the other states emerging from the Northwest Territory and the national government. These new states were granted the same powers as the older states, reflecting a shift of authority to the new American citizens. The thirteen original colonies wisely relinquished control of what was destined to become a vast nation, prioritizing the country's growth and the well-being of its citizens over disputes over governance.

The early settlers envisioned a nation where all citizens could contribute to the creation of a new society using their skills and interests. As the future states were admitted one by one into the Union, the Northwest Territory filled out with Ohio, Indiana, Illinois, Michigan, Wisconsin, and Minnesota. Ohio emerged as one of the most populous states in the country. Notably, eight of the next ten presidents hailed from Ohio, including Benjamin Harrison, who, while elected from Indiana, was born and raised in Ohio and can therefore be considered a "Buckeye."

General Dwight D. Eisenhower commanded the army that crossed the English Channel, playing a crucial role in rounding up parts of the Nazi forces in France. Meanwhile, General

Patton pursued the Nazis through Belgium and Germany, driving them into the arms of the Russians. In this era of military transformation, General John Murray became the first general of the newly established military division known as the Space Department. This initiative drew upon the expertise of various prominent scientists, including Thomas Edison, who contributed to numerous technological advancements, and Henry Ford, who revolutionized manufacturing with the moving assembly line.

Kenton, Ohio's Frank Ellis, a teacher of binary mathematics, also played a significant role in educating those who built the early computers. Additionally, Senator John Glenn, from New Concord, became the first American to orbit the Earth in a spacecraft and contributed to lunar exploration efforts, alongside another American hero, Neil Armstrong from Wapakoneta, Ohio. Armstrong made history as the first man to set foot on the moon, planting the iconic American flag on its surface.

About the Author

$\mathcal{J}$OHN M. TUDOR HAS BEEN a practicing attorney in Kenton, Ohio and other Ohio cities for 63 years. He retired on December 31 2022. He has seen face to face the liberties that we still experience as citizens of Ohio and of the United States. John Tudor has published a previous book "We the People" which has been used as a reference by fellow professors at Lees-McCrae College in North Carolina and elsewhere. He is concern about the lack of historical content in local schools and particularly the lack of interest in history of Ohio and its major contribution to the national history.

Appendix

The Articles of Confederation

THE ARTICLES OF CONFEDERATION AND Perpetual Union was the first formal agreement among the 13 original states of the United States, formerly known as the Thirteen Colonies. This landmark document served as the nation's initial framework of government. The Articles were extensively debated by the Second Continental Congress at Independence Hall in Philadelphia between July 1776 and November 1777. On November 15, 1777, the Congress finalized the Articles, though they didn't officially come into force until March 1, 1781, when all 13 states ratified them. The core principle of the Articles was to preserve the sovereignty and independence of each state, creating a confederation in which the central government had very limited powers—only those that the former colonies had previously granted to the king and parliament. The` Articles provided a set of clear rules for organizing the "league of friendship" known as the Perpetual Union. While waiting for all states to ratify, the Congress functioned under the guidance of the Articles, conducting the nation's business by directing the war effort, managing foreign diplomacy, handling territorial disputes, and negotiating with Native American tribes. Once ratified, the Articles didn't significantly alter how the Congress operated. The body, renamed the Congress of the Confederation, retained most of its previous structures, and many Americans still referred to it as the Continental Congress.

However, as the Confederation Congress attempted to govern the rapidly growing states, it became evident that the limitations placed on the central government—such as difficulties in raising funds, assembling delegates, and regulating commerce—rendered it ineffective. These challenges culminated in events like Shays's Rebellion, highlighting the urgent need for a more powerful federal government. As these weaknesses became apparent, political leaders across the young nation began advocating for revisions to the Articles.

In September 1786, some states met to address the economic and trade barriers that were hindering interstate commerce, and soon after, more states joined in pushing for broader reform. This led to the Philadelphia Convention, convened on May 25, 1787. Initially tasked with amending the Articles, the delegates quickly recognized that the defects could not be resolved through mere amendments. They decided to create an entirely new governing document, which resulted in the United States Constitution. This decision went beyond their original mandate, but it was seen as necessary to create a stronger central government.

On March 4, 1789, the government under the Articles was officially replaced by the federal government established under the new Constitution. The Constitution created a much stronger federal system by establishing the office of the President, a federal judiciary, and clear taxation powers, marking a pivotal transition from a loose confederation of states to a unified nation governed by a strong central authority.

The Ordinance Of 1787 (Northwest Ordinance)

FFICIALLY TITLED **"An Ordinance for the Government of the Territory of the United States North-West of the River Ohio,"** the **Northwest Ordinance** was a significant legislative act adopted on July 13, 1787, by the Confederation Congress. This Congress, functioning as the one-house legislature under the Articles of Confederation, laid the groundwork for the nation's westward expansion through this ordinance.

The **Northwest Ordinance** established a framework for governance in the **Northwest Territory**—an area that would later encompass the states of Ohio, Indiana, Illinois, Michigan, Wisconsin, and parts of Minnesota. This critical document not only charted a government for the territory but also devised a **method for admitting new states** to the Union on equal footing with the original 13 states. Additionally, it included a comprehensive **bill of rights** that guaranteed civil liberties such as religious freedom, the right to a trial by jury, and the prohibition of cruel and unusual punishment, all extended to settlers of the territory.

Following the **principles outlined by Thomas Jefferson** in the earlier **Ordinance of**

1784, the Northwest Ordinance's framers—likely **Nathan Dane** and **Rufus King**—crafted a visionary plan for the orderly expansion of the United States. This plan provided a blueprint that would be replicated as the country grew westward toward the Pacific Ocean.

The ordinance contained **three principal provisions** that would shape the development of future U.S. territories:

1. **Governmental Structure**: The ordinance established a temporary government for the Northwest Territory, with an appointed governor and judges to maintain order and enforce laws. As the population grew, a more representative government would be formed.

2. **Admission of New States**: It outlined a clear, step-by-step process for admitting new states into the Union once a territory's population reached a certain threshold. New states would enjoy equal status with the original states, ensuring that the Union would grow without a tiered or unequal system of governance.

3. **Prohibition of Slavery**: The ordinance famously prohibited slavery and involuntary servitude in the Northwest Territory, setting a precedent for the spread of free states in the northern United States. This provision would have far-reaching consequences in the decades leading up to the Civil War.

By codifying principles of civil liberties, equality among states, and the restriction of slavery, the Northwest Ordinance not only laid the foundation for the orderly settlement of new territories but also reinforced ideals that would echo throughout American history. This document is considered one of the most influential pieces of legislation passed under the Articles of Confederation, and it remains a testament to the foresight of the nation's early lawmakers.

The United States Constitution and Amendments

WRITTEN IN 1787, RATIFIED IN 1788, and in operation since 1789, the United States Constitution stands as the world's longest surviving written charter of government, representing the enduring principles upon which the nation was founded. Its opening words, "We The People," assert that the government's authority derives from its citizens, establishing the foundational idea that the United States government exists solely to serve the people. This affirmation of popular sovereignty is further emphasized in Article I, which establishes a bicameral legislature consisting of the Senate and the House of Representatives—demonstrating the priority placed on Congress as the "First Branch" of the federal government.

The Constitution outlines Congress's critical responsibilities, including the organization of the executive and judicial branches, raising revenue, declaring war, and crafting the laws necessary to execute these powers. Though the president holds the power to veto legislation, Congress retains the authority to override vetoes with a two-thirds majority in both houses, ensuring a system of checks and balances. Additionally, the Senate plays a crucial role in offering advice and consent on key executive and judicial appointments and treaties, further reinforcing the balance of power between branches.

For over two centuries, the Constitution has remained in force due to its brilliant design that effectively separates and balances governmental powers, protecting the interests of both majority rule and minority rights, as well as liberty and equality. The document's structure safeguards the relationship between federal and state governments, ensuring that neither entity oversteps its bounds. More than just a detailed operational guide, the Constitution is a concise declaration of national principles that has adapted to meet the demands of a rapidly evolving society, profoundly different from the 18th-century world in which it was created.

This adaptability is reflected in the 27 amendments that have been added to the Constitution, with the most recent being ratified in 1992. Notably, the first ten amendments, collectively known as the Bill of Rights, enshrine essential liberties and protect individual freedoms, further cementing the Constitution's role as a living document that continues to guide the nation in the pursuit of justice, equality, and democracy.